Starboortz Fish

This Book Belongs To

_____

Story Inspired by Neal Boortz
Nationally Renowned Radio Talk Show Host

Starboortz Fish

Written by
Barbara A. Hughes

Illustrated by
Elizabeth J. Clark

To Mom and Dad who taught me to read – B.A.H.
To Allison, Ashley, and Jeffrey, my three art critics – E.J.C.
Special Thanks to Mrs. Wynn and her Pre-K,
and
Ms. Mary, Judy M., Diane B., Janet I., Linda S., the Wauis,
and of course, Lexi

ISBN-13: 978-0-9792946-0-0   ISBN-10: 0-9792946-0-6

For information about our books and to order more copies
www.starlitpublishing.com

Third Printing
STARLIT PUBLISHING LLC

Printed in the United States of America

Deep in the ocean a fish stretched in the sand. This fish was not just any fish, this fish was a star. But, unlike other stars, this starfish did not shine brightly. In fact, he did not shine at all.

Starfish loved to talk to all the other fish.
"Good morning, good morning beautiful fish!
Let's see who is here today! I see striped fish and
solid fish, fish with short noses and long, long noses.
Hey there, Mr. Raccoon fish! You can't hide behind
that mask. I see you."

The other fish thought he was boring so they named him Starboortz Fish. That didn't stop Starboortz. He loved to hear his voice.

One day a smart old seahorse stopped to talk.

"Starboortz, all you do is blah, blah, blah! If you are such a star why don't you shine?"

"Well, you are a horse, aren't you, Curly Tail? Let's see you gallop."

But before the seahorse could answer, a huge blast of water came up and he floated away.

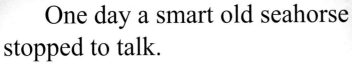

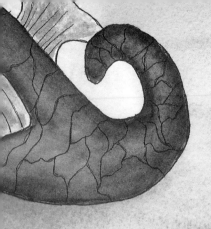

Starboortz thought about what Curly Tail had said. I am not a star because I don't shine. Well, we'll see about that!

He was in a deep sea of thought when he spotted something shiny.

"Hey, what do we have in here?" SPLAT!

"OH, NO!"

Starboortz was spattered in gold dust.

"Look! Look! I'm shining! I'm shining!" Starboortz shouted.

Curly Tail hitched up to the coral reef next to him.

"What happened to you, Starboortz? Having a bad hair day?"

"You're just angry because I shine now, but you still can't gallop," Starboortz answered.

The seahorse laughed, "Well, your *shine* is floating away!"

That night Starboortz sniffed back a tear.
He gazed toward the heavens. Against the
deep blue of the sky Starboortz searched all the
glistening, twinkling stars. He spotted the brightest
light in the night sky, his cousin Sparky.

"Sparky, I'm a starfish but I don't shine. Will you give me some of your sparkles? I want to shine like you."

Sparky's bright light flickered.

"I can't make you sparklc. I was born with my shine, but you must earn yours. Use what is special about you to shine."

"Once you have earned your shine, you
will be brighter than any star in the sky."
And with that advice, Sparky's light faded in
the early morning sun.

How can I earn my shine? Starboortz wondered for days and days and days.
"What is special about me?" he said aloud. He could not find the answer.

He decided to ask the old seahorse. "Curly Tail, what is special about me?"

"Well, all I know about you is your blah, blah, blah," the seahorse replied.

"Of course, of course! You are right, Curly Tail! It's my beautiful voice."

"No, No, that's not what I meant......!"

TOO LATE! Starboortz couldn't wait to show the other fish how he could shine.

He shouted with his voice, "Attention! Watch out Sergeant Major fish!"

He whispered with his voice, "Sh-h! Look at that little baby Lionfish. Isn't she cute?"

He sang with his voice, "La, la, la! This little voice of mine will shine, shine, shine!"

Curly Tail could stand it no longer.
"Starboortz, what are you doing? I can hear your voice all over the waves. You are giving everyone a headache! All you do everyday is blah, blah, blah, and la, la, la!"

"Sparky told me I could earn my shine if I used what is special about me."

"Well, Starboortz, you aren't going to earn anything. No one is listening."

A tear fell from his face. He covered his eyes. How could he earn his shine if no one listened to him? He quit talking. He did not whisper. He did not shout. He did not sing.

One day as Starboortz quietly watched the fish, he saw a shark with a mouthful of big white sharp teeth after them.

"YIKES! SWIM! SWIM FAST!!!" Starboortz shouted. "WATCH OUT, BABY LIONFISH! He is right behind you!"

"Hide in the cave! He won't be able to get you!"

Every fish could hear him. They slipped into the cave safely away from the huge shark.

The next day the fish stopped to talk to Starboortz. "Thank you for saving us! Without you that shark would have had us for his supper!"

"That's why they call him a starfish!" Curly Tail piped in. "You earned this, Starboortz." Then he hung a shiny medal around Starboortz and galloped away.

After that day you could hear Starboortz's voice above the ocean waves.

"Watch out, don't get tangled in that seaweed."

"Oops, QUICK! Hurry! Someone call Swordfish to cut him out!"

"No more danger in sight, but don't let your guard down."

Starboortz loved the sound of his voice and now so did all the other fish.

That night Sparky looked down from the heavens and saw a brilliant shine. Sparky smiled. Starboortz was not just any starfish, he was the brightest starfish in all the ocean.